Made in the USA
Las Vegas, NV
18 October 2024

96938021R00057